JAN WAHL

My Cat Ginger

pictures by NAAVA

TAMBOURINE BOOKS   NEW YORK

Text copyright © 1992 by Jan Wahl
Illustrations copyright © 1992 by Naava
Printed in Hong Kong by South China Printing Company (1988) Limited
Book design by Golda Laurens

Library of Congress Cataloging in Publication Data
Wahl, Jan.   My cat Ginger/by Jan Wahl; illustrated by Naava.
p.   cm.   Summary: A child describes all the special
attributes of Ginger the cat.
ISBN 0-688-10722-2 (trade).—ISBN 0-688-10723-0 (lib. bdg.)
[1. Cats—Fiction.]   I. Naava, ill.   II. Title.
PZ7.W1266My   1992   [E]—dc20   92-31883   CIP   AC

The illustrations were painted in acrylic on board.
1   3   5   7   9   10   8   6   4   2
FIRST EDITION

To Jeff and Buster Kitten
JAN WAHL

To Y.T.
NAAVA

My cat Ginger is
the smartest cat.
At night he lets me
use part of the pillow.

"Wake up," says
Ginger in the morning.
He washes his face.
And I wash mine.

He eats cat food
from a blue bowl.
I eat cornflakes
from a red bowl.

Ginger looks out.
He wants to be
where he isn't.

On rainy days,
we stay indoors.
I use my Build 'Em set.
Ginger helps me.

On sunny days,
we roll on the grass.
Ginger hopes
to catch a feather.

Sometimes he goes away
the whole night.
I put on my bathrobe.

I stand at the door
and call his name.
Snails slide on gray stalks.
"Did you see Ginger?"

Frogs sit by the pond.
"Did you see him?"
If they did,
they won't tell me.

I stop and think.

Maybe he jumps
in a flying saucer
and lands on
the hook of the moon.

He dances a jig
and howls a song
about shooting stars.
I'll bet he does.

In the morning I hear
a little sound.
"Where were you?"
'Nowhere," he purrs.

After lunch
we race to the meadow.
Ginger hides behind
some buttercups.

Now it's my turn.
He passes the bush
where I am hiding
and runs off to the stream.

He's too quick!
Zip—he's gone
around the bend.

I stop and think.

Maybe he hops on
a ship with tall sails.
His whiskers wiggle
in the breeze.

Another ship comes with
a thousand mouse pirates!
He takes up his sword.
I know he does.

This time, he's gone
two whole days.
At last . . . he returns.

"Were you in danger?"
"Ho hum," he answers.
Ginger takes a nap
on his rag rug.
I pretend to nap too.

He rubs against me
as if to say,
"No more nap.
Let's go for a ride."
So—off we go.

I love the smell
of cat breath.
Hey! Suddenly Ginger
leaps out and away.

I can't find him.

The woods make shadows.

The grass is tough and tangled.

I hear queer noises.

I stop and think.

I know just what happened.
Tigers chased him
high up in a treetop.

Wherever he is,
Ginger will not come down.
That night I pray,
Don't let him be hurt.

Then soon—can it be?
"I thought you were lost!"
He purrs and says nothing.

Before the sun is up,
Ginger howls to go outside.
This time I follow.
It's not easy.

He crawls through a pipe.

I scramble over a fence.

Now and then

he stops and waits.

The woods are thick.

I can feel the dew.

The sun rises.

I am quiet as anything.

I see where Ginger

has been going.

Seven babies lie hidden
on a soft, mossy bed.
The mother cat licks them.

Ginger looks proudly
at each and every one.

And we walk home,
my cat Ginger and I.